THE TURTLE INVASION

JACK PATTON

SCHOLASTIC INC.

With special thanks to Adrian Bott

ISBN 978-0-545-94518-9

10 9 8 7 6 5 4 3 2 1   16 17 18 19 20

Printed in the U.S.A.   40
First printing 2016
Book design by Phil Falco and Ellen Duda

CONTENTS

FLINT AND FIRE

Max Darwin strode through the forest as if he were back on Bug Island. The trees weren't quite as big, and his friends were human instead of giant talking bugs, but the feeling of being in the outdoors was just the same.

They were hiking on a woodland trail, heading toward the Boy Scout hut where they would spend the night. It wasn't far from Max's home, but it still felt like an adventure.

Up ahead, two of Max's fellow Scouts were singing as they marched in line. Suddenly one of them, Danny Grey, let out a yell.

"Whoa!" he cried as he stumbled over something on the ground. "What is that thing?"

"Max will know," called Chris Hollands. "Hey, Max! What is this? Some kind of a bug nest?"

Max hurried to see what they had found. In his path was a large brown mound, bulging up from the path like a little mountain. Danny's sneaker had made a deep mark in its side.

"Oh, that's bugs' work all right," said Max, fascinated.

"What kind of bugs?" Chris asked.

"I think it might be ants." Max bent down to take a closer look. He picked up a twig and prodded the mound carefully. Danny and Chris leaned in, too.

A moment later, both boys jumped back with a yell. A stream of scarlet ants came pouring out of the mound, flowing like lava down the side of a volcano.

"Not just any ants," Max gasped. "Fire ants! We need to leave these guys alone."

"Why?" Danny asked. "What are they going to do?"

"*Sting us,*" Max said. "They're called fire ants for a reason. They've got a lot of venom in those little bodies, and it hurts a lot. Trust me, I know."

Danny held up his hands. "Okay, I believe you! Come on, let's catch up with the others. I don't want to get left behind."

Together they hurried to join the other Scouts, who were gathered up ahead outside the hut. They took their places sitting on log seats around the empty fire pit.

"Okay, guys," called the Scoutmaster. "What I'm about to show you is one of the most important techniques you'll ever learn, especially when it comes to survival in the wild."

"How to find the nearest burger place?" Danny joked.

"Better than that. You're going to learn how to start a fire without matches. There are lots of different ways, but we're going to start with good old-fashioned flint and tinder."

The Scoutmaster directed them to gather up flints and dry grass from the forest floor. Max excitedly made a heap of grass and piled up flints alongside it. The Scoutmaster handed out pieces of char cloth, which was specially preburned linen. "Nothing better for turning a spark to a flame," he insisted.

Then, under the Scoutmaster's careful supervision, the boys tried to strike sparks using their steel penknives and the flints. Some of the boys managed it right away, and rewarding wisps of smoke began to rise from their grass piles. Max, however, couldn't make a single spark.

The Scoutmaster frowned down at Max as he scraped and scratched away with his flint and steel. Only one measly spark popped out, and it pinged off into the under- growth, where it fizzled and died.

"I can't seem to get the hang of it," Max grumbled.

"Hmm." The Scoutmaster frowned. "Maybe try a different way. What about the burning glass?"

"Burning glass?" Max asked, confused.

"You use a magnifying glass to focus the sun's rays. It makes a hot spot, and if you're lucky, you can blow it alight once it starts to smolder." The Scoutmaster patted his pockets. "Now, where did I put that magnifying glass of mine . . . ?"

"Don't worry. I've got one!" Max's magnifying glass had come with *The Complete Encyclopedia of Arthropods*, his magical book that was the gateway to Bug Island. The book was also an amazing store of bug knowledge. He pulled his backpack open and fished around inside.

"Uh-oh," the Scoutmaster said, peering in. "Looks like you've left your flashlight on, Max. You'll run down the batteries that way."

"Flashlight?" Max blinked, confused.

"Look. Something's shining away in there . . ."

Max looked down into his backpack, which was lighting up like fireworks on the Fourth of July. But it wasn't a flashlight that was glowing in there. It was the pages of his bug encyclopedia!

The Battle Bugs of Bug Island are sending me a message, he thought frantically. *They must need me!*

"I'll be right back," he told the surprised Scoutmaster, snatching up his backpack. "I think I left something in the Scout hut . . ."

Safely indoors, he tugged the encyclopedia from his bag. He took the magnifying glass from its pocket and quickly turned the pages until he found the one he was looking for. He laid the encyclopedia open

in front of him, showing the map of Bug Island.

He held the magnifying glass over the map and looked through it. The landscape changed before his eyes, turning from the color of ancient paper to the rich, vibrant green of grass. The island stood out in 3-D, from the cliffs to the bay, with a great stretch of rainforest in the middle.

Suddenly, Max felt a familiar force snatch him off his feet. The room around him seemed to swell and swirl. He went tumbling down into the book, heading into the map that was no longer a map, but the breathtaking reality that was Bug Island.

SHORTCUT

Max landed with a thud. His sneakers crunched on gritty, sloping rock and skidded out from under him. With a yell, he fell on his backside and slid even farther down the slope. With one flailing hand he caught hold of a rock and hung on to it until he'd stopped sliding.

"Ouch," he yelled as he came to a bumpy halt.

He struggled to his feet and dusted himself off. It was always a bit of a bumpy landing on Bug Island, but this time was even harder. The rocky slopes of Fang Mountain were not exactly a feather bed.

Max looked out at the amazing view over Bug Island. In the dim light of the morning, everything was calm and quiet. He listened for the telltale sound of crickets and other bugs, but he couldn't hear a thing.

The silence gave him a creepy feeling, as if he'd arrived too late for some important battle.

"Weird," Max whispered to himself. Part of him was relieved. At least he wasn't in the middle of a vicious reptile assault. The recent bird raid was still fresh in his memory. Bee-eaters loaded with flying Draco lizard troops had almost overwhelmed the Battle Bugs, and only Max's quick actions had saved the day.

"Better make my way to Bug Camp," Max said to himself. "They'll know what's going on." He looked down and saw the forest stretching out below him. Farther off to the south, he could make out the curve of the bay, and then the forest, where the bugs usually lived.

The only way to reach the forest was to descend the slopes of Fang Mountain, and Max didn't have a bug's advantages when it came to climbing. He picked his way down the gentler slopes easily enough, but the steeper drops were more treacherous. He hunkered down on his hands and knees, spreading his weight out as evenly as he could so he wouldn't fall.

Max was soon sweating from the effort of the hike, and the forest didn't seem to be getting any nearer. What he needed was a lift from a flying friend, like Buzz the hornet air ace, or even Alexis the giant butterfly.

He came to a halt on a rocky ledge and peered over the side. Then, he saw something that would help him: hanging vines dangling downward, looking as thick as rope.

"That's more like it." Max grinned. "Time to take a shortcut!"

Max took hold of a length of vine and braced his feet against the rock face. He remembered rappelling the indoor climbing wall with his Scout troop, and gently lowered himself down the rock wall, taking care to keep a good grip on the vine.

He glanced down as he climbed. The ground looked very far away, and the breeze made him swing in the air. Below, he spotted a narrow rock ledge with a little tree sprouting from the cliff just above. From there he might be able to make his way down to the forest.

However, as he pushed off the rock face with his legs, the vine made an ominous creaking noise. Then came a cracking, splitting sound.

"Uh-oh," Max cried. "I'm only half-way down!"

He frantically tried to climb down faster, but it was too late. The vine broke free from the side of the rock with a dry rattle of falling earth.

"Argh!" Max cried as he fell. In an instant he tumbled through the air and crashed through the branches of the little tree below. Before he could get his bearings, the branches split, and he went crashing to the rock ledge. The vine rope landed on top of him in a loose heap.

"Owww," he yelled for the second time this morning. "What's with today?"

He pulled himself upright again, wincing. The narrow ledge had even less room to move than he'd had before, and although he'd thought it might be easier to reach the forest from here, the sheer drop below made his heart lurch. He was stuck, he realized, with no way down and no way back up.

"Looks like you're trapped, strange bug," hissed a sinister voice from behind him.

Max spun around, his heart thumping in his chest.

"What the—" he began. But as he looked, all he could see was the tree he'd crashed through and the rocky mountain face. He narrowed his eyes and peered closer. He could've sworn the voice had come from near the tree.

"Over here," he heard the voice tease. "Or am I over here . . . ?"

Max whirled back and forth, trying to find where the source of the noise was coming from. Suddenly, he didn't have to wonder anymore—the bark of the tree blinked, and before his eyes, the tree seemed to move.

It was a lizard! And it was staring hungrily at Max.

Max gasped in fright. The lizard was dark brown and green, with gnarly scales that looked just like a tree trunk. It was the most amazing and terrifying camouflage he'd ever seen. In an instant, he knew what kind of lizard it must be.

"You're a mossy leaf-tailed gecko!" he exclaimed.

The gecko looked at him curiously. "What I am, little bug, is no concern of yours. Though you are right about my proud gecko heritage." It angled its head thoughtfully. "Why are you here? I thought all the bugs had retreated, like the cowards they are."

"I'm no coward!" shouted Max.

The gecko chuckled. "That's what they all say. But the moment they see the general coming, they soon run and hide."

Questions raced through Max's mind. Could the Battle Bugs really be hiding? And who was this "general" the gecko thought was so scary?

But there was no time to wonder about

all that, as the hissing gecko came charging straight toward him.

"You're going to wish you'd hidden away like all the others!" it snarled.

Max jumped back in fright. He had to find a weapon—any weapon. The fallen vine was still coiled at his feet. On impulse, he snatched it up and whirled the loose end around his head, making a thrumming noise.

"Come any closer and I'll make you wish you hadn't," he yelled. The tough, flexible vine would make a pretty handy whip.

The gecko paced around him, hissing. Max flicked his vine whip at it and hit it in the head. The gecko staggered back.

"A lucky shot," it snapped. "But your luck is about to run out!"

It sprinted at Max, weaving to the left and right. He struck out with his vine whip, but the nimble gecko dodged out of the way. In the next second, the gecko was upon him. Clammy, sticky claws shoved him up against the rock face. Max struggled in the creature's powerful grip, but it was too strong.

"Any last words?" gloated the gecko.

Uh-oh, Max thought, feeling panic overwhelm him. *There's no way out of this one . . .*

But suddenly, a distant, familiar droning noise reached his ears. Then he spotted something darting through the trees, something he recognized—and he knew he had a chance.

"Last words?" he yelled. "How about . . . *eat this*!"

With that, he head-butted the gecko right on its nose.

The gecko squealed and clutched its face. With one last surge of energy, Max flung the lizard away from him.

As it writhed on its back, struggling to right itself, Max sprinted toward the tip of the ledge.

"Silly bug," the gecko seethed, pulling itself upright. "You can't survive that drop. You'll be killed."

"Oh, yeah?" Max grinned. "Watch me."

Max took a deep breath and flung himself over the edge with a wild whoop. In an instant, he was plunging down toward the forest floor, hundreds of feet below.

BUG HIDEOUT

Max felt the air whoosh through his hair as he fell. The ground loomed up before him, coming closer and closer with each passing second. In moments he would be a boy-sized splat on the forest floor.

"Any time now would be good!" he shouted, hoping the bug he needed would hear.

Suddenly, the stripy figure of Buzz, the

hornet commander of the Battle Bugs air division, came into view. Max spread his arms out wide and did his best to steer himself into her path. With pinpoint precision, she buzzed under him, wings whirring ferociously. Max landed right on top of her, gripping on to her bristly back.

"Caught you!" Buzz cheered. "Welcome back to Bug Island, Max."

"Thanks, Buzz. I knew I could count on you!"

The bold hornet whizzed back up through the sky until she was higher than the treetops. She flew past the ledge Max had just jumped from. The mossy leaf-tailed gecko glared at Max with bugged-out eyes. It hissed angrily and flicked its tongue—but it was no match for Max and Buzz, who were soon out of sight.

"See you later," Max teased.

Max clung on tightly as Buzz rocketed through the air, banking and swerving so hard he was nearly flung off her back. He wrapped the vine rope around his waist. It might come in handy again.

Buzz shot past the barren, rocky mountain peak and made straight for a flat area slightly lower down. It was still high above the ground, but instead of being bare and rocky, it was overgrown with leafy plants and tangled greenery.

Good visibility, Max thought, *and easy to defend, too. If I had to choose, that's where I'd put a bug hideout.*

The Battle Bugs had clearly gotten the same idea, because as Buzz came in to land, Max noticed bug constructions all around. But they were so basic, it looked like the wasps and termites had needed to make them in a hurry.

A half-collapsed fort stood at the edge of the plateau. Buzz touched down beside the wall and bowed her head so Max could climb off. As he did, he saw three familiar figures emerge from the shadows: Spike the emperor scorpion, Webster the trap-door spider, and Barton the titan beetle, commander of the Battle Bugs.

"Well done, Buzz!" said Barton. "I was worried our message had reached Max too late."

"No, just in time," said Max, a little out of breath. The breakneck flight had left Max a little unsteady, and he leaned against the wall to regain his balance.

His head soon cleared, but something still felt odd. He patted himself down, trying to figure out what was different. A heavy weight had been pressing on his side, but now it was gone.

"The magnifying glass!" he groaned. "Oh no. I've lost it!"

He frantically checked his other pockets, while the Battle Bug commanders looked on with concern.

"It must have fallen out of my pocket on the flight over," he gasped.

"Sorry," said Buzz, wiggling her antennae. "Maybe I should have gone slower."

"It's not your fault," said Max, meaning it. He felt like kicking himself. How could he have lost something so precious? It was irreplaceable—and more importantly, it was his only way back to the real world.

"Max, I'm afraid there's more bad news," said Barton. "We are all in grave danger. While you were away in your world, the lizards attacked in force, in far greater numbers than any invasion we have ever seen before."

Max looked around at the half-built camp. "So what the gecko said was true? We're in retreat?"

"Those lousy reptiles overran the main

camp in the forest!" Spike cried. "They busted through our defenses and broke down our walls, and of course we fought them, but they just kept coming!"

"We lost the camp?" Max asked, his voice sounding hollow. It hardly seemed possible. The bug fortress had been mighty, like a towering castle. "But without the lava bridge, how could the reptiles bring enough troops across from Reptile Island?"

"Sea turtles," said Barton darkly. "They're even better at carrying troops across the water than the alligators. There were thousands of reptiles in the first wave alone."

Max was shocked. Bug Island was all but conquered. And with the magnifying glass lost, he was stuck here, too.

"We're n-not giving up, though," said Webster. "All over the island, the b-bugs are regrouping their forces, ready to fight back."

Max nodded, glad the bugs still had their fighting spirit. "So what's the plan?"

"Many of the surviving bugs have gone underground," rumbled Barton. "I'm planning to use the tunnel system under Bug Island to make tactical strikes against the reptiles."

"But there's a problem," Spike butted in. "Only Glower knows the complete layout of the tunnels, and he's been taken prisoner again."

"Where is he now?" Max asked.

"Glower never made it out of the camp," Barton said. "He stayed and fought while other bugs ran for their lives. When we last saw him, he was being carried off by a team of lizards."

"In that case, we have to rescue him," Max said, clenching his fists.

"All right, short stuff," Spike said. "Let's get to it!"

Quickly, Max and Spike set off. As the sun steadily rose in the sky, they descended the mountain. Being on Spike's back was a lot steadier than riding on Buzz, though it was still rough going, especially when Spike went charging off down near-vertical slopes.

"Whoa!" Max yelled, as the scorpion took a bend too fast.

"Hold on, partner," Spike cried, scuttling down the gravelly slope. Max tried to dig his heels in, but they just scuffed against the surface. Spike scrabbled and clutched like a spider trying to escape from a bathtub.

Eventually they came to rest, sideways, at the foot of the slope.

"Well, that's one way to get down the mountain fast," gasped Max. "Come on, buddy. Let's get to the old camp."

Together, they stalked their way between the massive trunks of trees and across the leaf-laden ground. Max usually felt safe here, but not today. He kept glancing around, alert for any sign of reptiles. Creatures like the leaf-tailed gecko could be hiding anywhere. You wouldn't see them until you were right up close, and then it might be too late.

Spike hunkered down as they approached the ruins of the camp. Only his stinger showed above the scattered leaves, poking out like the periscope of a submarine.

Max flinched as he saw the shattered remains of the once-proud bug camp—the place was in ruins. What mattered now was getting Glower out, so the resistance could begin.

"Should I get closer?" Spike whispered.

"Wait here a minute," said Max. "Listen up."

Soon, Max could just make out several hissing voices coming from the camp, as the reptiles argued among themselves. He poked his head above the leaf cover and caught a glimpse of some of them. A gang of sea turtles was boasting about the number of reptiles they had all ferried across the ocean, while a Western fence lizard with yellow spots bragged about the fighting he'd been in.

A tokay lizard, thought Max. *Another kind of gecko . . . and a big one, too.*

"You should have seen me!" it said. "Smashing bugs to the left and right! I took down that Barton, all by myself!"

"Don't lie," hissed a sea turtle. "Barton escaped. Everyone knows it."

"Nah. That must have been a bug-double," mumbled the tokay lizard. "I got Barton. I got that scorpion, Spike, too."

Max had to hold Spike back from charging in and attacking on the spot. "Keep listening," he whispered. "We need intel."

The biggest sea turtle roared with laughter. "You think you've seen fighting, little lizard? Just you wait until the next wave of turtles arrives at sundown. Then you'll see a battle to end all battles!"

Max's ears pricked up and he urged Spike closer. But just as the scorpion edged forward, Max saw something that froze the blood in his veins. A monstrous head reared up over the crumbling battlements. It was sleek, like a dragon—which, in a way, it was.

It was a beast Max had faced down before. Last time he'd seen it, it had been roaring in anger as it was swamped by a tsunami.

"You did not destroy Barton, soldier," it snarled. "None of you did, and none of you will. Barton is mine!"

"That voice," Max whispered. "It's him."

"But it *can't* be," said Spike.

"It is. It's General Komodo!"

THE RETURN

Max's mouth hung open. "I can't believe it," he whispered. "How can General Komodo possibly be alive?"

He thought back to the mighty battle for Bug Island several months earlier. The lizard army had mounted an all-out attack, and most of them had managed to swarm onto the lava bridge that had connected the two islands. Just as all had seemed lost, the volcano on Reptile Island, known to the lizards as the Great Reptilicus, had erupted. The bridge was swept away, and Komodo went with it—or at least that's what they'd thought.

"Spike, tell me I'm not seeing things!"

"Keep your voice down," warned Spike. "They said something about sea turtles landing tonight."

But the lizard voices had already died down to a hush, as if none of them dared to speak in the presence of their general.

"You lazy reptiles should be interrogating the prisoner, not gossiping among yourselves," Komodo snarled. "If I catch you . . ."

He stopped midsentence. Max crouched, trembling, and watched Komodo crane his huge head toward them, peering through the trees.

His forked tongue flicked out and in, out and in, as if he could taste the air.

What's he up to? Max wondered. Then, he realized. *That's how he smells his prey . . . prey like me!*

"We are being watched!" Komodo roared. "Spies are in the forest. Find them!"

"Let's get out of here," Max said. He wheeled Spike around and galloped the scorpion back into the surrounding forest. They plunged into the deep foliage, where bright flowers towered above them like skyscrapers.

Komodo came lumbering after them, crashing through the undergrowth and bellowing. The tokay lizard, eager to prove itself, went racing ahead in front.

Max glanced over his shoulder and saw the huge komodo dragon right on him.

"Faster, Spike! He's catching up!"

Spike scrabbled through the fallen leaves while Max clung on. General Komodo bounded after them and made a flying leap.

Max let out a yell as Komodo's claws grabbed hold of him and he went tumbling to the ground.

As Max writhed on the ground, the tokay lizard sprang into action, chasing Spike farther into the jungle. In an instant, Max was left on his own.

Like something in a nightmare, Komodo waded toward him. He looked like a rampaging dinosaur. As Max peered up from the forest floor, he realized that there was only one way out of this. There was a tree above him. Its surface was covered with wrinkled bark that looked like it might be easy to climb. He pulled himself up and made a break for it, grabbing handholds and footholds as he went.

Steadily, Max inched his way up the tree, as Komodo bellowed with rage behind him.

"Don't you know when you're beaten?" roared Komodo. "I'm coming for you, worm!"

On an impulse, Max looked behind him—and immediately wished he hadn't. General Komodo began to rear up on his

hind legs and shake the tree with his huge claws. Max clung on as best he could, but Komodo was shaking so hard the bark was coming away from the tree.

Komodo paused, peered at the branch, and laughed. "So many times you have been my nemesis, and now I have you trapped, clinging to a tree like a fat little caterpillar!"

"You're supposed to be dead!" Max shouted.

"I'm delighted to disappoint you," sneered the reptile. "You came close to finishing me, I admit. Closer than any bug ever has. But the tsunami was not enough to kill me, human. And nothing can keep me from my destiny . . . to conquer Bug Island!"

Komodo lunged and struck with his claws. There was a violent sound of tearing wood, and the tree branch broke clean off. Max, who was still clinging to it, went hurtling to the ground.

The impact knocked the wind out of him. He lay on his back, fighting for breath. General Komodo's leering face loomed huge in his vision. Then there was nothing but darkness.

It was still dark when Max awoke. He had to fight hard to make his eyes adjust to the dim light. He looked around him and could tell he was inside a termite tower—or what had once been a termite tower. The entrance was blocked up with a huge scoop of mud, no doubt plastered there by a sea turtle.

The only light in his gloomy cell came from a crack in the wall, far too small to squeeze through. Max pressed an eye to it and saw lizards patrolling back and forth outside.

"Komodo's keeping me prisoner," he muttered to himself. "That's not good. But it's better than being eaten. There's got to be some way out of here."

"Well. This is a familiar feeling, isn't it?" asked a dry voice from the corner of the room. "Last time we two were trapped together, it was in Lieutenant Titan's cave."

A light flared to life. Max saw that it was the luminous body of an old friend.

"Glower!" he cried. "Am I glad to see you!"

"You too, Max," said Glower, the firefly intelligence specialist.

"This was supposed to be a rescue mission," Max began. "But, um, things didn't exactly go according to plan."

Glower's firefly body glowed bright in agreement. "They never do, young Max!" He edged close and lit up the entire chamber.

"The reptiles seem to be saving us for something," he said. "If they don't want to eat us, then they must want information."

"I could use some information myself," Max said. "How can Komodo be back? I thought we'd beaten him."

Glower checked over his shoulder and then drew closer to Max.

"Well," he began. "From what I overheard, he's been resting up on Reptile Island, secretly coordinating the other attacks, and letting the other lizards do the dirty work. But since they've all failed, he's decided to come back and take over the island for himself."

"One thing's for sure," Max said. "If we don't get out of here, we'll be eaten, and the remnants of the bugs' forces will be destroyed."

"I'm afraid you are correct," said Glower.

Max hunted around, looking for a way out. The crack in the wall was narrow, but he thought he might be able to widen it enough to squeeze through. He took a fistful of earth and tugged it away.

Immediately, a gecko's eye appeared at

the crack. "You in there!" snapped the gecko. "Back away from the wall. No funny business!"

Max sat down heavily on the floor. "It's no use, Glower. Those guards don't miss anything."

"I'm not surprised they are diligent, what with Komodo himself watching over them," said Glower. "No doubt he will devour any of his troops who fail him today."

There's no way out, Max thought. *There are reptile sentries standing all around this stump of a building.*

Then an idea came to him.

"Glower?" he whispered. "Instead of finding a way *out,* maybe we can find a way *down.*"

ESCAPE!

"Termites built this tower," Max whispered excitedly, "and if I'm remembering right, termites always build an emergency exit!"

Back when the termites had built the watchtower on the Howling Cliffs, the fore-man had shared a secret with Max: *There's always a secret exit, just in case . . .*

"You mean to say there's been a way to escape this prison all along, right under my antennae?" said Glower, flickering with excitement.

"There's only one way to find out!" Max replied.

With mounting excitement, Max and Glower searched around the dingy cavern. They ignored the walls and poked at the floor every few steps, checking to see if the packed mud-and-dung mixture felt different anywhere.

Sure enough, Max's foot soon crunched against a leafy mat, similar to what Webster used to seal off his burrows.

"Glower, over here! I think I've found it."

Between them, they lifted the trap-door as quietly as they could. Underneath lay a narrow tunnel plunging down into the darkness. Max gave Glower a silent thumbs-up.

"Excellent fellows, those termites," said Glower. "Follow me, Max. I'll soon have my bearings."

Glower was as good as his word. They had not gone far through the tunnels before Glower cried "Aha!" and pointed out a little cave opening.

An emergency shelter stretched out in front of them. Stockpiles of sticky nectar for food lay in one—plenty to see the bugs through if it was too dangerous to go back to the surface.

"It sounds like it's occupied," Max said. He could hear the sound of chittering bug voices from inside the shelter. By the sound of it, there were thousands of them in there.

The pair of them went to investigate. By the light of Glower's glow, Max saw rank upon rank of bugs huddling in the cave: mantises, ants, beetles, and even some flying bugs, like the tarantula hawks.

"Max!" shouted a mantis. "You're alive! Welcome to Bunker 8-U-G."

The bugs crowded around Max, eager to tell him all about the battles they'd fought. One cicada chirped about the camp being overrun. A scorpion boasted about stinging a dozen lizards.

"I'm glad to see so many of you made it," Max said. "Are you ready to fight again?"

"YES, SIR!" bellowed the assembled bugs.

"Great. Okay, here are your orders. Nobody is to go above ground until sundown. That's when the lizards are planning their next attack. When the moment comes, I want you all to gather at Fang Mountain so we can defend the beach."

"Roger that!" said the mantis, giving a salute.

Glower tapped Max on the shoulder. "We should visit all the bunkers, if we can," he said. "There may be more bugs we can rally."

"Good thinking!"

Farther down the tunnel, they came across the entrance to Bunker 4-N-T. It turned out to be full of bullet ants who were delighted to hear there was more fighting ahead.

"We'll be there at sundown," snarled the bullet ant commander, snapping his mandibles and flexing his stinger. "About time you bigwigs in Battle Bug Command gave us something to do!"

"Wow," muttered Max as they moved on. "He was antsy."

"Well, yes," agreed Glower. "He's an ant. It goes with the territory."

They moved on through the tunnels, visiting every bunker they found on the way. One of them was sheltering a swarm of bees, whose queen promised Max the support of her troops. Another was literally crawling with spider troops. Max was growing exhausted when he finally spotted a shaft of light up ahead.

"Glower, I think we're at the surface!"

"This tunnel will take you up to the forest," Glower said. "Good luck, Max. I have to leave you here."

"You aren't coming with me?"

"There are more bunkers I need to visit. Every bug needs to know the battle plans, so our armies can act as one. I can do that work on my own. You, I think, are needed elsewhere."

Max nodded solemnly and shook Glower's extended foreleg. "See you soon, old buddy."

"We'll be sipping nectar together on Fang Mountain tomorrow morning," Glower said. He sounded like he wanted to believe it.

Max saluted, and hurried up the tunnel and out into the bright light of day.

Alone among the vast trees of the forest, he tried to get his bearings. The sound of splashing water was coming from some- where close by. Max ran toward the noise, glancing around for reptile scouts. No scaly eyes watched him as he passed.

He soon found himself standing on the banks of a rocky stream that cut straight through the forest. The splashing was com- ing from a nearby waterfall, where strange, bright flowers bobbed in the mist.

Max threw some cold water on his face, clambered onto a rock, and tried to see where he was. Away to the north he could make out Fang Mountain, while to the south lay the long, sandy beach and beyond it, the sea. Max imagined how it must look from above. The river neatly cut off the southernmost patch of forest that lay beside the beach.

He turned his attention to the odd flowers by the waterfall, and the rocks that glittered under the water's impact. Then he stopped and looked more closely at the foaming water. Something was gleaming up from the streambed—something he'd been afraid was lost forever.

Max was suddenly very glad he still had his vine rope. He unslung it, tied one end around a nearby tree, and the other end around his waist. He gave it a tug to make sure it was secure, then waded into the churning waters.

"I can't be too careful in running water," he panted. "Not since that time General Longtooth nearly swallowed me whole."

The water came up to his shoulders, but the vine rope held him steady. He took a breath and dived down, groping in front of him for the glittering object.

He came spluttering to the surface, holding the shining thing triumphantly as a trophy. It was his missing magnifying glass, still miraculously intact.

Just as he was beginning to think his luck had changed for the better, he flinched in sudden fear. A gruff voice boomed out behind him:

"Hey! What do you think you're doing in there?"

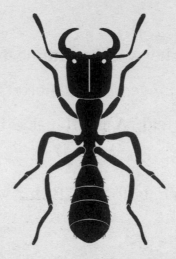

BUGS, ASSEMBLE!

Max staggered back through the deep river as a shadowy form loomed up in front of him. Water made his vision blurry, but he could tell the creature was dark-colored, large, and very agitated.

"Hey!" it shouted again. "Max! What do you think you're doing? Going for a swim? Come out of there before you get swept away!"

"Spike?" Max gasped. He rubbed the water out of his eyes and saw it was only his scorpion friend, fidgeting anxiously at the stream's edge.

"What's this? A vine?" Spike tugged at it. "I'll pull you out."

Spike hauled Max up out of the stream. Just as he managed to stagger onto the bank, Spike launched into what had happened with the tokay lizard.

"As soon as I noticed you had fallen off, I turned around and went looking for you," he said, sounding a little embarrassed. "But the tokay lizard followed me all through the forest. I managed to sting him, but when I turned back to you, I couldn't find you!"

"No worries." Max laughed. "At least you got back at that lizard."

"I was so mad!" Spike clashed his pincers. "Anyway, I'm glad you're in one piece, short-stuff. Barton's got to be going buggy, wondering what's become of us. We need to get back to the camp, fast."

The mountaintop camp, which had been almost deserted before, was heaving with bugs. Glower's message had been passed on all across the island, and now thousands of bug warriors were getting ready for the final battle.

Barton was pacing nervously back and forth when Spike and Max arrived. "You made it!" he shouted, sounding very relieved.

"Glower made it, too," Max told him. "He's heading to all the underground bug bunkers, letting our troops know what to do."

"It's a good thing he did," said Barton. "Buzz and her air scouts have informed me that the sea turtles are already on their way across the water."

Max gasped. "But the attack isn't supposed to come until sunset."

"Komodo clearly wants his troops in position ahead of time," Barton said. "We need to act fast!"

"Then let's assemble our own troops," Max said.

Together, Max and Barton went and spoke to the leaders of the various bug battalions. "The most important thing is to decide where everyone's going to be," Max explained. "If there's no plan, there'll just be chaos and Komodo will steamroll us."

"What's a steamroll?" Barton asked.

"Never mind. I think we should put the stag beetles on the front line, since they have heavy armor. Scorpions on the flanks, mantises in reserve to drop in from the air, and burrowing bugs under the sand for a shock strike."

"I have a newly trained battalion of fire ants ready to go," said Barton. "You haven't met them yet. They're itching to get into the fight."

Max stopped. At the mention of fire ants, an idea had popped into his head.

Fire, he thought. *I wonder . . .*

"Max?" Barton said, peering closely at him. "Are you all right?"

"More than all right, General," Max said slowly. "I think I know a way to get rid of the reptiles once and for all."

"IS THIS RIGHT?" boomed Dobs, the giant dobsonfly, as he dumped a heap of dry grass by the edge of the forest.

"Perfect!" called Max. From his perch on the rocky banks of the river, he watched the bugs work. Their project was coming along nicely. The giant dobsonflies and some helpful termites had made several piles of twigs, dry grass, and parched bark, all of them directly beneath large trees.

"I'm not sure what good you think this will do, Max," said Buzz irritably. "These heaps of stuff won't stop the reptiles. They'll just climb right over them!"

"Trust me," Max insisted. "What I have in mind will definitely stop the reptiles. We just need to make sure we have things set up along the path of the river."

"I'm on it," Buzz said. She rocketed up into the air.

Barton tapped him on the shoulder. "I, ah, have to say, Max, I still don't understand what you have in mind . . ."

"I'm confused," added Spike. "You know I don't like being confused!"

Max sighed. "I'm building a weapon I hope I won't ever have to use. It's a defensive measure of last resort!"

ANT WARRIORS

Once Max's mysterious defense was in place, Barton flew up into the air to address the troops.

"The rumors you have heard are true," he shouted. "General Komodo has returned. Over the past months he has skulked like a coward, letting other reptiles carry out his plans for him. Now he has finally shown his face. Well, my brave friends, I call upon you all to kick Komodo's scaly tail back to Reptile Island!"

The bugs all cheered. Max rode on Spike's back at the head of the bug forces. Following Max's lead, the bugs marched forward through the forest. Many of them were still making their way down the mountain, streaming down the sides like shiny, blackish-brown lava. The sound of hundreds of thousands of bug bodies moving through the leaves was like the rushing of a mighty river.

"I just hope it's enough for us to win," Max muttered.

"It'll have to be," said Spike.

The forest floor beneath Spike's many legs gave way to sand and matted grass, and the trees became sparser. Max sat up straight, braced to fight. They were nearly at the beach. He ducked under a low-hanging branch and brushed a large leaf out of his path.

Something heavy thumped into him from behind. He fell from Spike's back, yelling and lashing out with feet and fists. The creature that had hold of him hissed and snapped its jaws in his face.

It was a mossy leaf-tailed gecko—and Max was sure it was the same one that had cornered him on Fang Mountain. The same hungry leer was in its eyes. The reptile had been clinging to the branch Max had just passed under, and the "leaf" had been its tail!

"Don't move," the gecko said. "And tell your scorpion to back off, or I'll crunch you up like a mouthful of ants!"

Spike hovered his stinger over the gecko—he was about to clamp downward, but realized that if he struck, he might get Max instead of the gecko.

Max struggled, but the gecko's sticky grasp was tight as a knotted rope. "Get off me!" he yelled.

"I don't think so," hissed the gecko. "You're a hostage now, human. Your forces won't dare to attack while I have you at my mercy!"

The gecko shoved Max down against the ground.

Max twisted in pain, but then he heard something—the sound of scrabbling legs and clicking mouthparts. It was coming from *underground*, and it was getting louder all the time.

"What?" demanded the gecko. "What are you smiling about?"

The forest floor underneath Max erupted. Just like when he had poked the mound back in his own world, a stream of ants poured up through a freshly dug hole.

Max's grin grew wider as he saw they weren't just any ants. They were the bullet ants he'd met down in the bunker, and Max knew they had a very painful sting.

"Gecko in sight!" yelled the bullet ant leader. "Ant warriors, engage!"

The startled gecko didn't have time to react. The bullet ants swarmed all over it. Because they were so much smaller, many of them could climb onto the gecko at once.

Then the stinging began. The gecko yelped in pain, let go of Max, and went hobbling off toward the beach.

Max stood up and dusted himself off. "Thanks for the rescue. It's good to see you again."

"Thank your firefly friend. He told us where you'd be," said the bullet ant captain.

"Glower!" Max yelled, running over to where he was climbing out of the hole.

"It looks like we were just in time," Glower said. "Come on, Max. There's a battle to fight and a war to win."

With military precision, the bugs marched down to the beach. The beetles formed the main brunt of the army, with the scorpions, centipedes, and spiders backing them up. Close by were the mantis shock troops, and overhead buzzed a giant cloud of hornets, bees, wasps, and other stinging flyers. Barton strode along in the very heart of the army, surrounded by his elite fire ant soldiers.

Max caught sight of Komodo's head, looming over the sand dunes.

"There he is," Max called out.

"He won't get away this time," Spike said.

Komodo dragged his huge, heavy body to the top of a sand dune and looked up and down the bug ranks. His tongue flicked out, tasting the air.

"General Komodo!" Barton called out. "We bugs fight with honor, so I am giving you one chance to surrender. If you don't, certain defeat awaits you!"

Komodo stared, and then burst out laughing. "You've taken too many knocks to the head, Barton! Certain defeat? Oh, no. This time I have Bug Island in my grasp." He looked back over his shoulder and bellowed, "Invasion force, advance!"

Max felt ice water running in his veins as he saw the first of the sea turtles emerge from the crashing waves. The creature was terrifying enough in itself, with a gnashing beak and flippers that could crush legions of bugs, but even worse was the load it was carrying. Clinging to the sea turtle's back like an ugly growth was an entire battalion of common lizards. Battle hunger gleamed from their eyes.

The turtle lowered its head and the lizards swarmed down onto the beach, using the head like a landing ramp.

Then the next sea turtle pulled itself ashore, and then the next, one after the other until the beach was crowded with them. Almost every one carried a group of reptiles or amphibians on its back. Max saw vipers, skinks, iguanas, monitor lizards, chameleons, and even little newts slither into position.

As the blood-red sun sank into the sea, the lizard army grew and grew. Max realized that General Komodo really was playing for keeps this time. He had staked everything on this one battle, and he did not intend to lose.

The two armies faced one another.

Barton took a deep breath. "Battle Bugs, attack!"

The massive bug army surged forward, crawling across the beach and onto the dunes. The reptiles roared and charged to meet them.

Max whipped his vine rope around his head, ready to lash out with it. Spike thundered over the sand alongside the bee-tles, heading straight for the oncoming reptile forces.

The two armies crashed together. All along the front lines, fierce fighting broke out. Lizards bit and clawed at thick beetle armor. Hornets zoomed down from the sky, struck with a barrage of stings, and then soared away out of range of reptile jaws. Snakes hissed and lunged at writh-ing centipedes. Mantises lashed out at fat frogs.

From Spike's back, Max fought as hard as the rest. He thwacked lizards with his vine whip, knocking them onto their backs so Spike could sting them. Although the pair of them were practiced fighters, and stunned reptiles soon lay groaning all around them, they struggled to make any headway against the oncoming tide of Komodo's troops.

"There's too many of them, Max!" grunted Spike, grabbing a lizard in each claw and bashing their heads together.

"Keep fighting," Max yelled. He looked around to see how the battle was going, and felt like his heart had fallen right out of his chest.

The bug forces were being driven back. The sea turtles, though slow, were unstoppable. Nothing the bugs did could pierce their thick shells or their tough hide.

"Max!" Barton called. "We have to do something!"

Max nodded gravely. There was only one option left now.

He turned to the bugs and gave the order.

"Battle Bugs, retreat!"

SECRET WEAPON

Max watched the brave bugs turn and run. The faster ones, like the spiders, raced away over the dunes and vanished into the forest.

"Air division, help the wounded!" ordered Buzz.

Flying bugs rushed in, grabbed their buddies who were too injured to walk, and flew them away from the reptile advance. Barton himself flew straight past Komodo's nose to rescue a submerged mantis.

"No bug left behind," Barton said firmly. He snatched the mantis up in his huge pincers and carried him away. Komodo snapped at them, but Barton easily dodged him.

"Run, you pathetic bugs!" Komodo roared. "It will do you no good. Wherever you hide, we will find you and devour you. We have won!"

Max wheeled Spike around. "Battle Bugs, follow me. Make for the forest."

With Max leading the way, the bug army went into full retreat. They charged away from the beach and through the trees. Some of the bugs headed for the shelter of the trees and began to climb up them, but Max yelled at them to stay out. "It's safer on the ground, trust me," he said.

The reptiles pursued the bug army, but to Max's relief, they weren't moving as fast as he'd feared. Komodo and his sea turtles lumbered slowly across the sand, and he understood. Komodo's troops didn't dare to attack before their general—Barton was his.

The shadow of a tall tree fell across them. Max knew that tree well. Earlier that day, he'd assigned a group of termites to it to do a very special job. He crossed his fingers for luck and hoped they'd been able to do the job in time.

"Termite squad," he called. "Are you ready for Operation Lumberjack?"

A termite stuck its head out of the side of the tree. "All set," it squeaked.

Max glanced behind him. The reptiles were coming, slithering, scrambling, and flopping from the beach and into the forest shade. They were advancing slowly and cautiously, as if they expected a trap. *Well, guess what*, Max thought. *A trap is exactly what you're walking into.*

"Now!" Max told the termites.

From inside the tree trunk came the noise of thousands of termite jaws munching at once.

General Komodo heard. He frowned and looked around. "Reptiles, halt."

There was a deep groaning, splintering sound. The horrified reptiles in the front line looked up to see that the tall tree was toppling down toward them. The termites had eaten right through it!

Max watched with satisfaction as the long, thick tree trunk crashed down right in the reptiles' path. It rolled a little way toward the beach, forcing them to dive out of the way or be crushed. Then it came to rest, with the bugs on one side and the reptiles on the other.

"A cheap tactic, human," snarled Komodo.

"But it worked," yelled Max.

"Maybe. But not for long. Sea turtles, advance."

Max rode away from the reptile ranks

and headed for the river, as they slowly clambered over the fallen trunk.

The bug evacuation was in full swing. The flying bugs were ferrying as many flightless bugs over the river as they could carry. Ant troops grabbed hold of one another and built bridges out of their own bodies, letting the retreating bugs climb over them. Spiders spun webbing lines over the water for other bugs to climb across. Some of the bugs were even sailing over the river, using broad, flat leaves as makeshift rafts.

Max rode Spike up to the rock he had used for a lookout post. His heart was pounding as he watched the reptiles scrambling over the fallen tree. They were coming, and he was running out of time. The bugs *had* to cross the river, every single one of them, or he wouldn't be able to put his plan into action.

"Step it up," he shouted to the bugs. "We need more bridges, right now!"

"Out of the way," roared a familiar voice. Max saw that the voice belonged to Gigantus, the giant centipede warrior he'd teamed up with before. She reared up her long, black, segmented body and lunged across the river at its narrowest point. Grateful bugs swarmed across her, using her as a bridge.

"Good job, Gigantus," Max said. "No bug left behind, right?"

"Right," grunted the centipede, straining under the weight of so many bugs. As the very last bug—a tiny aphid—limped over Gigantus's body to safety and the last reptile slithered over the fallen tree, Max climbed down off Spike's back.

"Time for the secret weapon," he whispered to himself. "I just hope this works."

He reached into his pocket and pulled out the magnifying glass.

Max could hear the reptiles crashing through the undergrowth, heading his way. He held the magnifying glass steady and focused the sun's rays on one of the heaps of dry grass.

A tiny, bright white spot appeared. A

wisp of smoke went up. In a flash, more smoke rose up, thick and white.

"Come on, come on," he said through gritted teeth. *"Light . . ."*

The reptiles were almost upon him now. Iguanas swiveled their eyes toward him and flicked their tongues out. Snakes glided stealthily through the dead leaves. Thousands of pairs of cold, merciless eyes watched him.

"Leave it, Max!" yelled Spike from the far side of the river. "Run!"

Max ignored him and kept the lens focused. There was a red glow in the pile of dry grass and the smoke was pouring out. Suddenly, Max knew what he had to do. He fell to his knees and blew gently on the glowing spot.

WOOMPH. Yellow flames licked up through the little dry heap. Max sprang back as a crawling circle of fire steadily spread out. The reptiles paused, uncertain as to what was happening.

Max ran back to his lookout rock. The fire was taking hold, and fast. First the forest floor became a rolling curtain of flames, carrying the fire from tree to tree. Then the trees themselves began to catch. It took only moments for an entire tree to be engulfed in flames. Max knew that the fire would be halted by the river—but for now, it created a fiery wall between the bugs and the lizard forces.

What had begun as a backyard bonfire was soon a raging inferno. Trees were transformed into blazing torches. Glowing cinders blew on the breeze, spreading the fire even farther afield.

Choked by the smoke, half-roasted by the heat, the lizards turned and ran.

"This is bug magic!" screeched a gecko as a burning branch crashed down in front of it. "The bugs have somehow tapped the power of the volcano, the Great Reptilicus itself!"

"Stand and fight!" bellowed Komodo. "That's an order!"

"Never mind your orders," croaked a sea turtle. "I'm not staying here to be cooked alive. I'll take my chances in the sea."

Flames danced in Max's eyes as he watched the reptiles run. Heat and smoke made his head swim.

"We've done it," he cried. "The lizards are in retreat!"

VENOM POINT

As the lizards retreated back to Reptile Island, Max turned away from the burning forest.

Through the billowing clouds of smoke, he could see the Battle Bugs on the far side of the river, waving happily at him. Webster was hopping on the spot with joy, Spike was applauding by clicking his pincers, and even Barton looked delighted.

"I'm coming, guys!" Max called. He climbed over the rocks toward one of the spiderweb bridges. *One sticky climb*, he thought, *and I'm safe.*

Before he could reach the web line, a huge clawed foot crashed down in front of him.

A hissing cry rang out: "Human! You have interfered with my plans for the very last time!"

It was General Komodo, somehow still alive. His scaly hide was blackened with soot and his eyes gleamed with hate. Max staggered back, filled with sudden fear.

Komodo charged.

Max could only turn and run for his life, gasping and wheezing from the smoke. He hopped from rock to rock along the river's edge while Komodo scrambled along behind him.

From the other side of the river, Max heard Barton shout: "Buzz, fly over and give Max an immediate evac!"

"On it!" Buzz replied.

While Max desperately tried to outrun Komodo, he heard the whir of Buzz's wings as she took off.

His allies' voices vanished into the distance. Smoke swirled around Max as he ran. From nearby came the crash and boom of burning trees toppling to the ground. Komodo's hoarse, furious roars assaulted his ears. Max's chest ached and his eyes were streaming.

"Got to keep going," Max gasped. He couldn't let Komodo catch him.

The drone of Buzz's wings grew louder and louder. Max looked behind to see the brave hornet powering through the smoke toward him. But to his horror, he saw she was in trouble. Instead of flying straight and true, she was wobbling around in the air.

"Buzz, what's wrong?" he yelled.

"It's this smoke!" Buzz cried. "I can't see where I'm going!"

As Max struggled to climb up the rocks beside the waterfall, he heard a sudden splash. He looked back to see Buzz tumbling out of the sky and into the river. Two fishing spiders immediately ran out across the water to rescue her.

I should have known, Max thought. *In the human world, people use smoke to confuse wasps and bees. No wonder Buzz couldn't handle it.*

"Your rescuer has fallen, and none of your bug comrades can reach you before I do," hissed General Komodo from right behind Max's shoulder. "Now it is just you and me, human!"

He's right, Max thought. *After so many battles, it's down to the two of us. A human boy against a reptile monster.*

He forced himself to run on. They were on the lower slopes of Fang Mountain now, where natural paths led up toward barren, craggy peaks. There was nowhere to go but up.

Every muscle in Max's body ached as he climbed, but there was no stopping now. Max hauled himself up stony slopes and grabbed branches to steady himself. Komodo pounded along, always right behind him, his feet sounding a *THOOM*, *THOOM*, *THOOM* on the bare earth.

Just as the nightmare chase seemed it would go on forever, Max came skidding to a halt. He saw that he had run to the end of a long ledge of rock that jutted out over Bug Island like a wasp's stinger. Beyond was a sheer drop that plunged down for thousands of feet. This, he remembered too late, was Venom Point, the precipice at the very top of Fang Mountain.

Komodo came into view. "Nowhere left to run," he wheezed.

Max wished like he'd never wished before that his magnifying glass would start to tug him into the sky and away from here.

But nothing happened.

He backed away farther across Venom Point until the heel of his sneaker scuffed against the very edge of the drop.

"What, do you expect to fly away to safety?" sneered Komodo. "You have no wings, human. No stinger, no poison, no pincers, no web. No special abilities at all. You are not even worthy to fight alongside the bugs. You are *nothing*!"

Max knelt down at the edge of Venom Point, next to a little dead tree that jutted out of the ground. Komodo's words had given him an idea. He hunched over, pretending to be out of breath—he hoped Komodo couldn't see what he was up to.

"Time to finish this," Komodo snarled. He opened his mouth wide and came charging right at Max.

Max held his ground, trembling all over, as Komodo rushed toward him. The reptile's mouth loomed up, gaping wide as a train tunnel. Max took a breath . . . and stepped backward off Venom Point.

Komodo charged forward, desperately clawing at the rock, but he was going too fast to stop. His arrogance had made him reckless. With a terrible cry, he stumbled off Venom Point.

Max dangled just below the edge, hanging from his trusty vine rope.

He watched Komodo fall and fall, until the reptile vanished from sight. Komodo let out a desperate cry but it was far too late—he would never be seen again.

I wish Webster could see me, hanging from my homemade web line, he thought. *I may not be a bug, but I've learned some of their tricks!*

From below, the bugs of Bug Island let out a hearty cheer. Suddenly, he felt something tug on his trusty vine rope. He hauled himself back up the side of the cliff face,

and was welcomed by Barton and Spike, and the other bug commanders.

"You did it!" Barton cried. "Bug Island is saved."

Max beamed with pride. The fire wall he'd created had done its job and was slowly fizzling out. From this vantage point, they could see the lizards fleeing back across the choppy waters between the two islands.

"So I guess that's it, short-stuff," said Spike.

"Until next time." Max winked. He pulled the magnifying glass from his pocket. This time it was glowing. He held it up to the sky . . . and before he knew it, he was rushed off his feet and into the air.

Back in the human world, Max came running out of the Scout hut. His little heap of kindling was waiting for him. The other Boy Scouts were all busy with their fires.

"There you are, Max!" said the Scoutmaster. "I was going to send out a search party."

"Have I been gone long?" Max asked.

"About ten minutes. Come on, let's see you get your fire going."

Ten minutes, Max thought with a grin. *If only they knew.*

Just as he'd done on Bug Island, he focused the sun's rays to create a point of burning heat. His char cloth instantly began to smolder. Max leaned in and blew the fire alight.

The Scoutmaster clapped. "Excellent work."

"Thanks!" said Max. He looked down at the tiny lick of flame he'd created, and quickly stamped it out again.

The Scoutmaster looked on approvingly. "Keeping fires under control prevents damage to the environment."

"I know," Max said with a smile, as he thought back to the burning forest on Bug Island. "And they can do much more than that!"

REAL LIFE BATTLE BUGS!

Fire Ants

"Fire ant" is the common name for over 200 species of ant, which can be found in diverse habitats across the world, from North and South America, to China and Southeast Asia. Although there are variations across the globe, they're primarily known for their red-brown coloration and their painful sting—hence the name!

Like other species of ant, the fire ant lives in colonies built into soil. These can usually be found under fallen timber or rocks and can occasionally be seen poking up over a foot above the ground. The colony is founded by a queen—who can live as long as seven years—and is supported by up to 250,000 workers!

Unlike other species of ant, which spray acid as a defense mechanism, the fire ant likes to get up close and personal. It has a specialized, alkaloid-injecting sting, as well as mandibles for biting. It causes a burning sensation and irritation to anyone unlucky enough to have been stung.

Bullet Ants

Bullet ants are a species of ant native to Central and South America. Their range stretches from lowland rainforest in Nicaragua all the way south to Paraguay. They build their colonies of 100–200 ants at the base of trees, and survive on a diet of tree sap and smaller insects.

They're famous for their incredibly powerful sting, which has been reported to be very painful. More painful than the paper wasp, the red harvester ant, and the pepsis wasp, its sting is supposedly as excruciating as being shot!

Given its amazing powers of defense, you might think the bullet ant would always get its own way—but it can also be a victim.

Bullet ants tend to use their amazing abilities against other bullet ants in battles for the best food and colony locations. Their battles are so ferocious, some ants end up wounded and vulnerable, which is when the phorid fly chooses its moment.

The phorid fly doesn't eat the bullet ant, though. Instead, the female of the species lays its eggs inside the wounded ant. When the time comes for the larvae to hatch, they have a ready-made meal waiting, and the bullet ant is eaten from the inside out!

LIZARD ATTACK!

The lizard's tongue shot from its mouth like a whip. Then, slowly, it lumbered forward. Max held his breath. It was gigantic. The ground shook with every stamp of its big, clawed feet.

"How nice of you to drop in," it hissed, "just in time for dinner."

Max gulped. From where he was sitting,

the lizard looked as big as a dinosaur. It could easily win a battle against the scorpion. As for the tiny human being on its back . . .

"Back off, you scaly bully," said the scorpion. It raised its stinger threateningly, ready to strike. The stinger's pointed tip was hanging right next to Max's head, a bead of white venom on the end. Max edged away from it, lying down as flat as he could and peering over the scorpion's eyes.

The lizard hissed. "I don't like it when my snacks fight back," it spat. It advanced again, backing the scorpion up against the branch they'd just climbed.

Max knew that the emperor scorpion was well armed. Its huge, powerful pincers and venomous stinger made it a dangerous enemy. But the lizard's scaly skin would be far too thick and tough for the scorpion's stinger to pierce.

There has to be some *way out of this,* Max thought, his heart pounding. *Maybe the scorpion can outrun it?* He looked at the lizard's powerful legs, and swallowed hard. Scorpions could run fast, but the alligator lizard looked quick, too, and it wasn't carrying a passenger.

The lizard opened its mouth, showing its sharp, pointed teeth, and suddenly leaped forward. Max clung on tightly as the scorpion scuttled to the side, dodging out of the lizard's reach.

The lizard turned slowly to face them, its yellow eyes glittering. Once again, it stepped closer. Then it stopped and tipped its head to one side.

"What do you have on your back?" it asked curiously.

Max looked up to see that the lizard was staring straight at him. The scales on its flat, crocodile-like head were all the same size, except around its nostrils, where they were smaller and darker. Suddenly, Max remembered something.

"Quick!" he whispered to the scorpion. "His scales are weaker around his nostrils! Use your pincers there!"

"Stop that whispering!" bellowed the lizard. "What sort of thing are you, anyway?"

Max glared back at the lizard. "I'm his secret weapon!" he shouted.

And with that the scorpion darted forward, taking the reptile by surprise. Before it could react, the scorpion snapped one of its pincers onto the lizard's nose. The lizard gave a high-pitched hiss and backed away, twisting its head in pain.

"Let's go!" shouted Max.

The scorpion charged around the lizard as it retreated, holding a clawed foot to its injured snout. But Max knew they weren't out of danger yet. The lizard might still come after them. And if it did, it would be even angrier than before.

The scorpion seemed to have realized this, too, because it was running as fast as its legs could carry it. "Thanks for the tip," it shouted back to Max.

JOIN THE RACE!

It's an incredible adventure through the animal kingdom, as kids zip-line, kayak, and scuba dive their way to the finish line! Packed with cool facts about amazing creatures, dangerous habitats, and more!

■ SCHOLASTIC

scholastic.com

MEET RANGER

A time–traveling golden retriever with search-and-rescue training . . . and a nose for danger!